THE FIRST VERSE

This book was written by Lawrence Britt

2 SWORDS

A tale of Two Swords: An Eclectic Fairy Tale.

Post War victory let me share a little history.

Not the beginning, not the end. This is the story of how we win. Father and son, their job is never done.

They fight to save the day, to protect the way. The ideal of heroes, always in the fray.

Hordes of fiends they must defeat, there is no one that can compete.

Their swords have been lost but not all is, there is nothing more frightening than this, while villains fight for chaotic bliss.

Those who hope for peace will not cease.

As they search for the swords of space and time, they will overturn every stone and leave nothing left behind.

This is how we win the fight.

This is how we win.

Turmoil

The swords are lost but not all is.

Not all is, there is truth in this.

The ceaseless above watches everyone he does not do this just for fun.

Keeping tabs, keeping score. Saving poor rewards for villains who know not what is in store.

He built a legacy a standard.

Instead of complaining your life you should be changing. For what is the cost, the wage to age and not bare fruit. You only get one shot so shoot.

Disbelief

Disbelief. It's not rare when you are in despair, you can feel it in the air. Almost taste it at times you no longer care.

But just one, he is not alone a collective rising looking for a new home.

Raised in the sewers the gutters the grates. Eating scraps off empty plates.

He stands in the muck, the mire, the clay. He looks to the ceaseless but not to pray.

He speaks, I will stand and rule the day.

Order

The one in the clay takes a name, he is no longer the same. No more mire, no more tears, he was stripped of all his fears.

His plate full, he is strong not willing to accept when he is wrong.

Sanity stolen along with love and hope, he believes now though but only that honor is a joke.

His fists start to harden much like his heart. His eyes and tongue sharpen only to pull people apart.

He gathers the others the parts that were left, he needs them together their worst is his best.

The First Blade

The first sword is clean and has a golden sheen. It looks unworn but through space it has ripped and torn.

It searches for a master to take it by the horn.

Its powers are vast and great I must say, so powerful any who wield it might fade away.

It travels through worlds and realms, with no one at the helm.

Its' strength does overwhelm.

Its powers are vast and great and when it finds an heir a throne it will make.

Roth One

I am the one from the sewer, from the gutter. My name is Rothel I will stand above all others.

From the clay and mire I rise. Not one soul stands to look me in the eyes.

From the plains and the fields, I do not yield. To forge my throne, a sword must I wield.

The King Maker

Soel is my name, dominions I build and tame as though it were a game. I have raised kings and similar things, I am the agent of change.

I've been poor and rich, I've always found a niche. I am the only constant pitch.

My power is not great I don't need it to be, I only need to influence one you see. Only one other and me.

I have chosen a child he is one of three and when I am done a king he will be.

He is one with no fee, no cost, he has no one to love no one to have lost.

You will know him well his name is Roth.

Domain

I am Rothel hear me speak, I will not
tolerate the weak. This tribe is strong and
mean, our strength has yet to be seen.

I will devour my foes causing them great
woe, my power, our power they will come to
know.

I do not do these things just for show.

I am real, and they will feel my power grow.

Black tears from pale eyes

Soel must I keep watching people die?

Yes, Roth you must, or when you eat, you will feast and instead of meat it will be dust.

But Soel I am tired.

Rothel keep pressing, keep the charge soon your tribe will be great, and your kingdom will be large.

Hold tight drink some tears, a sip of blood it can't be hard.

But Soel you sound mad, insane, all the lives and innocence I have slain. To eat or have a bed truthfully, I wish I was dead.

No. Rothel my boy your insane, you commit these atrocities while feeling this pain, I feel nothing not even shame. I only want for food not fame.

So, take your fill their eyes or yours. Only the black tears from your pale eyes are for me of course.

The first blade part 2

Again, it sings, through space and matter it swings. The hum the vibration of its song carries a great distance far and long. It does cry, it does wail to who has eyes that are pale.

The sword also cries to another, one who is much younger. He still has his father and his mother.

One song of salvation the other destruction, when it chooses a wielder the wielder will choose its function.

Two sons both raised with care. One heart is full while the other is bare, one taught to love the other not to care. One wants what he is owed the other wants what is fair. Both Chosen, both young and like the swords their journey has just begun.

Compulsion

The one, Roth ole pale eyes can hear the song
of the sword this feeling can't be denied.

Time again and again he tried, the song
driving him insane taking his brain on a
cosmic ride.

He knows it is coming, he will wait for his
sword his time he will bide.

Commander

Solvasse. He is not king, often a synonym for a beast with wings. He is strong he is wise. Clarity of mind to see through lies.

His brother a king maker one of many. They war for food but only hunger is plenty. He is looking for a group of warriors a band, an army that will take a stand.

He will lead, he will take command.

Wife

She is strong more important a mother a vessel of the cosmos that bares life for another. She teaches the young early on how battles are won. She loves her children both her daughters and her son. This mother, daughters are plenty, but as for sons she has one.

She will raise him to slay, to win to never yield she lends him her sword to wield.

Her war path is different more complex, the way she fights her style does vex.

The way of two swords she does teach, this art form her son must master, must complete.

Legacy

My mother trained me well, I will never fall
nor, have I ever fell. Surpassing limits and
breaking my shell. My power will grow I
will excel.

I'm young and meek.

I am small in stature, but I am not weak.

The enemies of liberty and freedom I do seek
their stories end with me their future bleak.

But Twelve

I am the legacy, the standard.

I will destroy evil, it is a cancer.

Solvasse is my leader, my teacher my commander. He is the reason we band together.

Practice

My name is Lorel many enemies I have fell.

With just a swing, a fling a graceful flick of the wrist of the wing of the edge of my blade, hear it sing.

The way my mother taught me.

The way the battle is won, fought you see.

When the odds are stacked against you, you make a decree a declaration of war. Then stand on your feet back against the wall and swing your swords.

It is sweet.

Lorel

My name stands for victory and so do I, I think my name had me in mind when it chose me and that is fine.

I will fall in line until it is my time to shine.

You want to see strength I will show you a sign.

I pray to the ceaseless for advice, he is always there to improve my life.

I will grow up strong and wise, look through evil and destroy its lies.

Dark webs of wickedness getting torn down. I scatter my enemies man look around.

There are none.

Solvasse

I have been chosen, my destiny woven. This is real not a dream. I used to answer to a man but now a king fate has made me it seems.

Maybe it is genetic, just runs in the blood, in the genes.

The path I have paved it was hard, it left my family scarred. But I followed my vision now I set the bar.

I was in command of a band of men, told them if they followed me I would show them how to win. Nothing has changed not now and not then.

Save for I am free, no longer a puppet, no more string. When I wake tomorrow I will be king.

Soel

My brother is going to be king, the people will probably cheer and sing.

He will get the crown with the mark and seal for his ring. But I'm his brother, the elder I make kings.

I pick crowns as though they were flowers. That is my ability, my power.

I think in advance and gain the upper hand by the hour. He cannot reign here, not this castle, it is my tower.

I will make him drink ale from the mead of life, the yellow sour.

Ruth

My husband is to be king, this is a marvelous thing. When no one is looking I will sneak away his crown and his ring. We will stroll through the royal garden and together we will sing.

The peace he will bring. The change of pace and life, he has made me a very happy wife.

My son when old enough can take command, he will get a small crew, a band. For this kingdom young Lorel will stand.

Together with his family.

Cry in the Void

A gnashing, a wailing.

The second ancient blade is flying, sailing.

Its path is imminent, divine. Its course is sublime as it crashes through time.

It is searching for a master.

It hears the cry of its brother and begins to move faster.

Warping time and reality, causing cosmic disasters. When it finds a home, a hand it will make a nest. It will only obey the best.

Second Blade

The second blade was made, not like its brother, it was not made with silver, nor like any other.

The second blade was made from jade, and when it would swing it would cast a bit of shade.

Its cry, its song would pulse and crush turning things into warped new things, from the ashes from the dust.

It too will find a user, simply because it must.

The name of the first blade

The name of the first blade is bleak and stark, its name is specter and it dances in the dark.

It uses its power for fame.

It loves the sound of its own name.

It destroys worlds just for games.

Its enemies are surely finished when it takes aim.

Destruction is its only function, it deliberately leaves scars on your soul just for punctuation.

When you hear its song, you should run.

The name of the second blade

The name of the second blade it sings.

Pulsing bursting through time and other cosmic things.

There is no wonder that reaper is its name. The power of the end of time and yet can still make change.

The shade it cast warps the past of the objects and celestial bodies it has passed.

When it finds a home, a throne all others it will outlast.

The previous war

The swords, the star bound brothers were not made for war. Unfortunately, they have fought and slaughtered until their edges were sore.

They needed something better, something more. They had destroyed so much they could no longer keep score.

So, when their master laid to rest, they ran away and set out on a quest. To find a new home a new throne for their best.

But they are broken, the fair used for their journey blood is the token.

They don't know their true voices, because death and destruction are all they have spoken.

Rothel

We will be victorious no one will ever come
close to us. We will turn and burn our
enemies to dust. Their kingdoms will fall to
ruin, to waste, to rust.

Soel

It must. We must eat, take the throne take a
seat.

Take the crown and destroy every city
around, look around not another more noble
is found.

That is why we will win.

The Kings Feast

Today is the day that the ceaseless has made a way.

Solvasse takes the throne.

The capital is now his home.

The kingdom will be safe.

Bring the food, the wine, the meat. It is time for the kings' feast.

The people will be safe, no more strife they can now live a peaceful life.

The After Party

The king was made.

No more fear, this was a time of joy and cheer.

He is quick and full of wit, he could lift his kingdom from the pit.

But he was tired and wanted to sit.

They should have never left the king alone, especially the first day on the throne.

There in the dark he can see the eyes, and unfortunately this is no surprise, at least the king went down swinging without a whimper or a cry.

He would leave his world with his head held high.

The after, after party

The king was dead this was a surprise, everyone was hurt you could see it in their eyes.

They were forced back to turmoil. Forced back to eating lies.

Their lives will get much worse Rothel and Soel will invoke the curse.

There will be evil everywhere you search. Even when you go home there a villainous fiend will lurk.

No cheer, applause, no more peace. From now on the war will not cease.

The black parade

This was no ordinary parade, it was a death march, a charade.

The new king started collecting tax early this year and there is no excuse that he would hear.

He loved collecting tax on his people's fear, he will take from them all their weight in tears.

The villain moved straight to his predecessors' home where his widowed wife and children sat alone.

But there was one, his single son he will not weep.

He stood alone outside practicing sword techniques, by the sheep.

The day the swords fell

Two suns and two sons. The battle has not
yet started. After this fight there will be no
one to cry for the departed.

The elder and his army stood against a bleak
existence, while facing the young man who
stood alone to defend his home.

Before the fight, a crowd was formed to see
this incredible sight.

But lo a sound.

A Cosmic ringing and two swords from
another dimension hit the ground.

The Choice

The swords wept and let out a whistle. They began to float and rolled along the ground as balls of thistle. Their sacred power so strong they scorched the earth into crystal.

The sword that bends space, time it did not waste.

As for the sword that crushes time it created a very specific line to make it to the hands of its wielder.

The one of destruction chose Rothel, the other chose Lorel.

The sword cloaked in time

As the two enemies stood, seemingly stuck in glue. Both fighters were whisked off as they and their swords flew.

The sky returned to normal, a heavy shade of green and blue. The bystanders stood in awe and looked as the chosen wielders departure left them covered in dirt and soot.

The sword cloaked in time was happy, it began to ring, sing and chime.

It would show his young master everything it knew and blow his mind.

The silver Sword

This sword pulled and dragged his master.

Through its own soul showing him all the chaos and disaster.

For a moment Rothel thought, it was better to make peace instead of fought.

Seeing all the ones the sword laid to rest he shed a tear.

For a moment he saw the swords true nature and his heart stopped out of fear.

The specter appeared

The show was over, Rothel was now sober. Him and his sword jutted back to his new home.

Rothel looked around no one else could be found, the sword had flung him all the way back to his throne.

The new powers within him he took and accepted, they were so incredible that he shuttered from the blessing. But inverted was a curse that will surely make things worse and soon enough his sins will need confessing.

Far from over

The sword of time heaved its master to and fro, where, when and would they stop no one would ever know.

It used its powers on Lorel to show just how much power they have and how much stronger they would grow.

Battles won and lost, warriors rise and fall.

The only one left to fight against this madness is Lorel, he will answer the call!

He will stand tall and the throne will be his, he has nothing to lose and everything to win.

Mean While

Mean while back in real time, we will find Rothel using his power to leave everyone behind.

Kingdom by kingdom they all fall down, now only one will wear a crown.

The battle horns blow in a shattering sound. The king and his blade are stuck, war bound.

Almost everyone defeated, this feat will never be repeated. Alas a few do stand against, to fight this evil a small band was sent.

This band of sisters, daughters of the old king, they were going to stop the new king so off they went.

Meanwhile part 2

The sisters would fight wise. They would fight hard at least they would try. They did not plan to die only to destroy Rothel with his lies.

But they were wrong, they could hear their own destruction in the form of a song, they wept as they knew their lives would not last long. Twas the song of the sword being sung by its master, the sisters were finished they met their disaster.

They were wrong

The sisters were wrong. They cried as they heard their funeral song, the chords were beautiful and lasted very long.

They came to stop the life Rothel led, they would find his broken truth instead.

The hungry nights with no shelter or bed. All the nights his now deceased siblings were never fed.

They had to eat it all, the fear the hatred. It no longer matters the sword will desecrate them. There is no one left to mourn, before the last is slain she cries in pain, I wish I was never born. Rothel whispers, what a shame.

The visitor

Soel sitting in a dungeon, a prison.

The guards circle by, stand him up he is risen. This is not how he expected his only blood son to treat him. Not at all did he expect that this is how he would be living.

His strength gone but it was something he never had, always relying on others wickedness how sad. He stood itching, wretched, sick picking at his skin that is scabbed clad.

When he breathes his last breath, he thinks he will be glad. But another breath he will never have because he stops when he sees Rothel descend, the sword has a price Soels son is the cost and Soels blood will be the currency they spend.

Yes, for the kingmaker this is the end. No more wills to bend. With one final stroke to the afterlife his soul was sent.

Alone

So much time has passed since we've seen our hero last. But the self-proclaimed villain Rothel sits alone on a throne and his kingdom is vast.

No one is here. It is mostly just fiends and other creepy things.

The people started a resistance but that was just to survive. With no wealth, no power, how much time can you buy.

Even most in the clandestine resistance are waiting, just to die.

Despair

Rothel sits alone, his gains leave him nothing to have shown. His wretchedness digs deep to the bone.

He wishes for youth and in truth a better life. Dreams for kids and a wife and simpler nights.

It is not over for him yet.

Not yet.

The Last Ride

His fate is final, his hands are tied.

He picks up his destiny and starts to walk and measure his stride.

He is not looking for the resistance, they no longer even hide.

No, today he will use his pale horse for his last ride.

His declaration by fate he will abide.

The Road Less Traveled

It is now this journey brings wisdom as his kingdom falls. It is only now that he realizes that he lost it all.

Beyond the ruins of the battle fields, beyond empty castle walls.

He reaches beyond the touch of man and senses something infinite at hand. He dismounts the horse to take a stand. He can feel that time begins to slow its sands.

This miracle marks the healing of the land.

The trees grow back and so does the grass, the rivers run strong and bass swim pass.

It would seem someone reversed the hour glass.

The Return

He is back, it is Lorel.

He picks up his blade and locks eyes with Rothel.

The putrid hate in the air can be smelled, the taste from the wasteland cannot be repelled.

Their gaze does not break, it seems to last for days. The two swords lash and gnash together, no longer traveling separate ways.

Now the cosmic brothers are together forever.

Lorel

It did not have to end this way, peace could have lasted all day.

For the lives lost you will now pay, it does not matter that you are old and gray.

For your life you should be ashamed, for your wrath you could not tame.

So now watch my sword take aim.

Rothel

Young man, little brother you can bet a soul
guarantee I have no regrets.

I've stood against everything against every
threat, I am the one that outlast I am the
vet.

You and no one else can hold their own, this
is my zone. I am the throne.

I will make quick work of you, so I can go
back to being alone.

The Odds

What are the odds, of it being us called to this path from the dust?

We stand to make war but not as brothers, not as friends.

It is a shame we cannot make amends.

So, I raise my sword to you, because I recognize your path as the truth.

This is what the two chosen declared to each other.

Their final battle begins with a nod.

What are the odds?

They Shine Together

The swords shine bright like stars in the night to them this is not a fight.

It is just a test. To see which cosmic brother is the best. They already know they are the better than the rest.

Their future means everything, now and then. They do not care who wins.

They will last forever.

Each time they will get stronger, better.

The Final Onslaught

The battle never easy, this war was long
fought both chosen warriors giving it
everything they have got. To not win would
be eithers only sin.

They do not yield the swords they wield,
with all their might and skill, absolutely no
chill. They swing and fling and display their
will.

All is on the metaphorical table before them.
Skills shown bright they toss and catch their
heavy tools on a whim.

Lorel gains the upper hand. A fling of the
cosmic blade, the clean sound of shwing,
drops Rothels head and he can no longer
stand. This is the end for him, but he won't
be remembered as a mere man.

He is a king a ruler, one that unites,
unfortunately his fate is to lose this cosmic
fight.

The Restoration.

The land was healed, evils fate was sealed.

Lorel is the strongest and so is his will.

Lessons learned the war is over, sin does have a cost.

Always choose to win, instead to have lost.

This is how we win!!!